MAJOR LEAGUE SPORTS

MAJOR LEAGUE SOCCER

By Derek Moon

Kaleidoscope
Minneapolis, MN

Your Front Row Seat to the Games

This edition first published in 2020 by Kaleidoscope Publishing, Inc.

For information regarding permission, write to
Kaleidoscope Publishing, Inc.
6012 Blue Circle Drive
Minnetonka, MN 55343

Library of Congress Control Number
2019939024

ISBN
978-1-64519-070-7 (library bound)
978-1-64494-159-1 (paperback)
978-1-64519-171-1 (ebook)

Printed in the United States of America.

TABLE OF CONTENTS

CHAPTER 1

Sebastian Blanco tied for the Portland lead in goals in 2018.

Derby Day

Sebastian Blanco waits. His Portland Timbers are on the move. Diego Valeri has the soccer ball. He races into the penalty box. A Seattle Sounders defender appears. He knocks the ball free. It's Blanco's time.

He gets the ball at the top of the box. A defender is on him. Blanco taps the ball with his right foot. The ball rolls behind the defender. Now Blanco has an opening. He chases the ball. He swings his left foot. The ball flies into the far corner of the net. It's a goal!

The crowd roars. This is a huge game. It's the **playoffs**. Portland is hosting its biggest **rival**. And now the Timbers are up 2–1. But a goal is just the start of the celebration in Portland.

An engine fires up. A buzz rises above the cheers. Timber Joey holds up a chainsaw. He is the team's **mascot**. He saws off part of a giant log. He gives the slab to Blanco after the game. It is one of many unique **traditions** in Major League Soccer (MLS).

SUPPORTERS' GROUPS

All sports teams have fans. In MLS, teams also have supporters' groups. The league recognizes more than sixty of them. Timbers Army is the biggest. It has more than 5,000 members. The fans stand together at Timbers games. Leaders direct them in cheers.

FUN FACT

The current Timbers are the fourth Portland soccer team to use that nickname.

Timber Joey fires up Timbers fans before a game.

Major League Soccer Map

1. Atlanta United FC
2. Chicago Fire
3. Colorado Rapids
4. Columbus Crew SC
5. D.C. United
6. FC Cincinnati
7. FC Dallas
8. Houston Dynamo
9. LA Galaxy
10. Los Angeles Football Club
11. Minnesota United FC
12. Montreal Impact
13. New England Revolution
14. New York City FC
15. New York Red Bulls
16. Orlando City SC
17. Philadelphia Union
18. Portland Timbers
19. Real Salt Lake
20. San Jose Earthquakes
21. Seattle Sounders FC
22. Sporting Kansas City
23. Toronto FC
24. Vancouver Whitecaps FC

Timbers Army unveils a tifo, a giant banner common in soccer, during a 2016 game.

Fans are a big part of MLS. Portland's stadium now seats more than 25,000 fans. But many of them stand. They aren't there just to watch. These fans are part of the action. Portland's fans are known for their passion. They sing. They chant. They wave flags. And on this day they cheered the Timbers to a 2–1 win.

Some even travel with the team. Many were in Seattle a few days later. The Sounders attract even bigger crowds. Their stadium is really loud. But Portland came through again. The Timbers moved on to the MLS Cup.

CHAPTER 2

Starting from Scratch

Eric Wynalda tapped his foot. He was nervous. So were his teammates. It was April 6, 1996. They were on the bus to Spartan Stadium. Their San Jose Clash were hosting D.C. United. This was MLS's first game.

The California skies were blue. A sellout crowd of 31,683 was watching. Wynalda was a skilled US forward. He could have played overseas. But he was excited to come home. One reason was to play in this game. But the game was sloppy. Neither team could score.

Then Wynalda made his move. It was the 87th minute. He got the ball. He **nutmegged** a defender. Then he ripped a right-footed shot. Goal! San Jose won 1–0.

FUN FACT

All original MLS teams were still playing in 2019 except for the Tampa Bay Mutiny.

Eric Wynalda, right, dribbles upfield in a 1996 MLS game.

A small crowd takes in the 1999 MLS All-Star Game in San Diego.

Some English teams have been around since the 1800s. The United States was just catching up. It had hosted the 1994 World Cup. Now it had a men's pro league. But MLS looked different in the early days. It had just ten teams. Crowds were small. But stadiums were big. Most teams played in pro football stadiums.

MLS began to struggle. In 2002, the league had to eliminate two teams. Some thought the league would not survive. But a new era was beginning. In 1999, the Columbus Crew had opened a new stadium. It was built just for soccer. Fans liked being closer to the action.

SOCCER FIELD

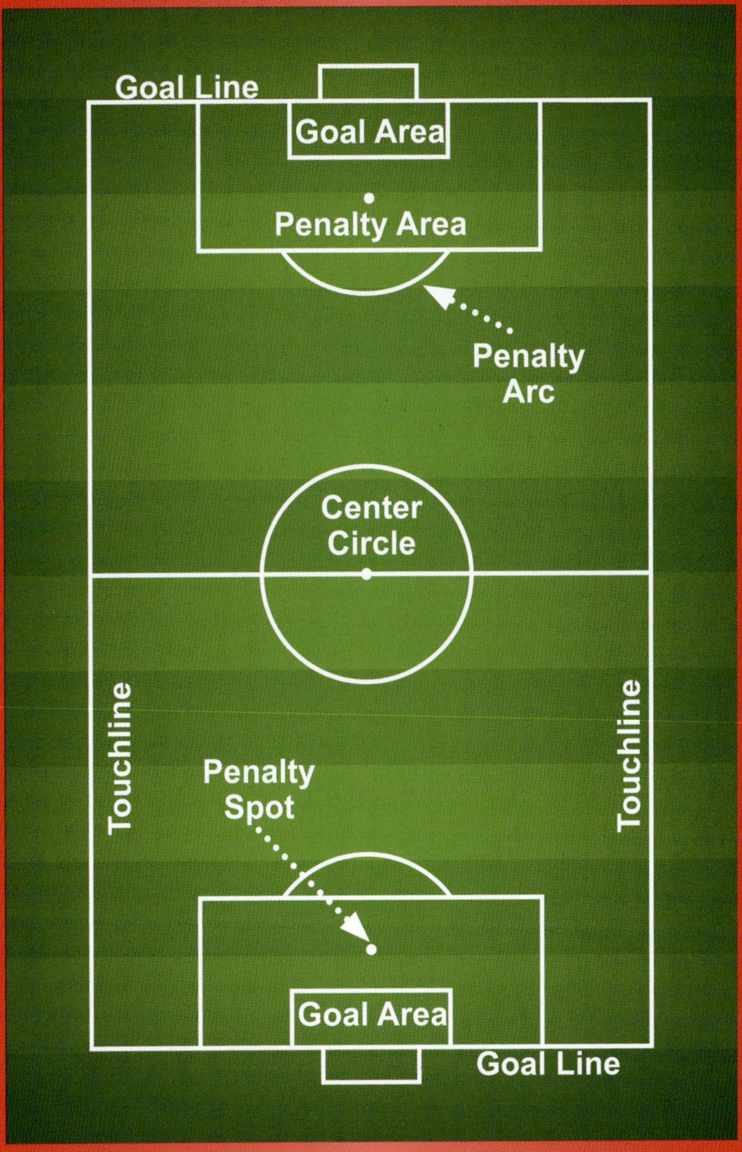

Toronto fans embraced their team right away, buying an MLS-record 14,000 season tickets in 2007.

Other changes were important, too. In 2007, the league relaxed its **salary cap**. This helped teams afford famous players from overseas. The league also continued to grow. In 2007, Toronto FC arrived. The team had its own stadium. Cheering fans filled it for every game. More new teams followed. In 2019, the league introduced its twenty-fourth team.

Toronto's BMO Field was centrally located and easy for fans to access.

CHAPTER 3

Beckham and Beyond

David Beckham was relaxed. He had played for some of the world's biggest teams. Big moments were nothing new. And this was one of them. It was the 2011 MLS Cup.

Beckham saw a pass coming up the field. He jumped to meet it. He easily flicked the ball with his head. Teammate Robbie Keane was streaking up the field. Keane took control of the ball. Then he passed into space. Teammate Landon Donovan filled it. He met the ball in the penalty box. He flicked his right foot. The ball looped to the right. The Houston goalie could only get one hand on it. Goal!

FUN FACT
The LA Galaxy sold 11,000 new season tickets after Beckham signed with them.

The Galaxy's Landon Donovan was one of the league's top goal-scorers.

D.C. United were MLS's first dynasty. They won three of the first four league titles.

The arrival of star player David Beckham in 2007 began a new era of MLS.

The LA Galaxy led 1–0. They went on to win the 2011 MLS Cup. A new era had begun.

Early on, MLS had a low salary cap. Some top Americans played in MLS. Forward Brian McBride was an early star. So was Carlos Valderrama. He also played for Colombia's national team. But MLS could not compete for the world's best players.

A 2007 rule began to change that. Some called it the "Beckham rule." Beckham was an English superstar midfielder. The rule allowed teams to sign a player above the salary cap. So the Galaxy signed Beckham.

MEXICAN STARS

Mexico has a strong league. Still, many Mexican stars have found a home in MLS. Goalie Jorge Campos came in 1996. He starred for the Galaxy. In 2007, midfielder Cuauhtemoc Blanco joined the Chicago Fire. Giovani Dos Santos and Carlos Vela came later. Dos Santos played for the Galaxy. Vela stars for nearby Los Angeles FC.

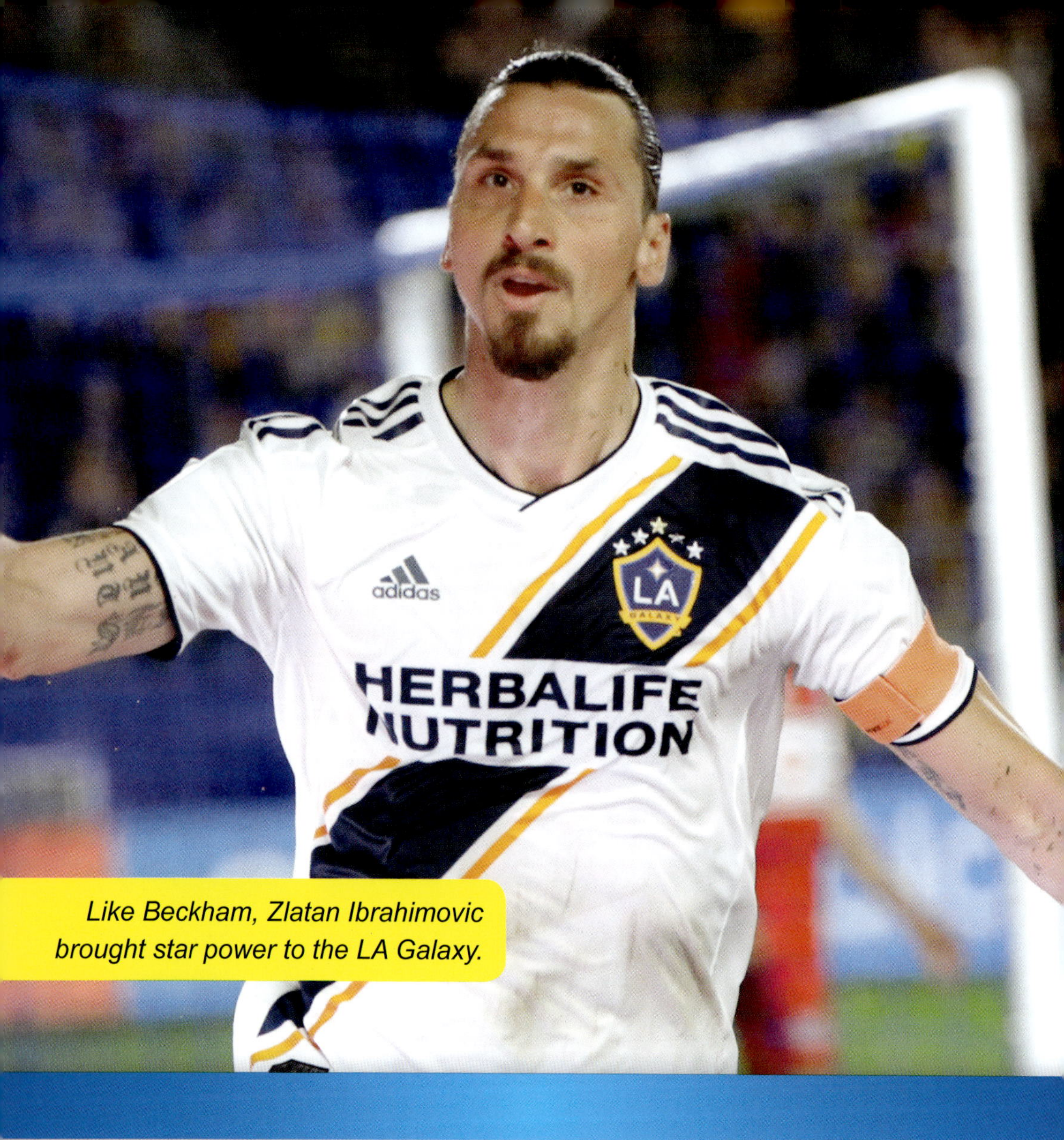

Like Beckham, Zlatan Ibrahimovic brought star power to the LA Galaxy.

It was not easy at first for Beckham. He did not know the league or its players. But he had Donovan. He was a top US player. MLS also relaxed more salary cap rules. So Keane joined them in 2011. The Irish striker was another big star. Together, these three lifted the Galaxy. They also showed that big-name players could succeed in MLS.

Other global stars followed. France's Thierry Henry was one. Brazil's Kaka came over. So did Spain's David Villa. Sweden's Zlatan Ibrahimovic arrived in 2018. Meanwhile, some top US stars made their home in MLS. Donovan, Clint Dempsey, and Michael Bradley were some of the biggest.

CHAPTER 4

Raising the Bar

One by one they arrived. There were men, women, boys, and girls. Fans of all kinds showed up in Atlanta, Georgia, in December 2018. In total, 73,019 fans took their seats. No MLS Cup final had seen so many fans. Most were there to cheer on the home team, Atlanta United.

Atlanta United supporters unveil a huge tifo before the 2018 MLS Cup.

The team did not exist two years earlier. Atlanta joined MLS in 2017. Immediately, it raised the bar. The team spared no expense. Atlanta signed talented young players. It planned to play in a fancy new stadium. And fans supported the team.

Josef Martinez gets around the Portland goalkeeper to score the first goal of the 2018 MLS Cup.

Atlanta made the playoffs in its first year. A league-high 48,200 fans showed up to home games. In 2018, the team was even better. That's how Atlanta found itself hosting the MLS Cup. The team faced the Portland Timbers.

Forward Josef Martinez was from Venezuela. He was one of Atlanta's key signings. And in the 39th minute, he struck. Martinez got the ball atop the penalty box. He was quickly one-on-one with the goalie. The forward cut to his right. The goalie was fooled. Martinez kicked the ball in for an easy goal. Atlanta went on to win 2–0.

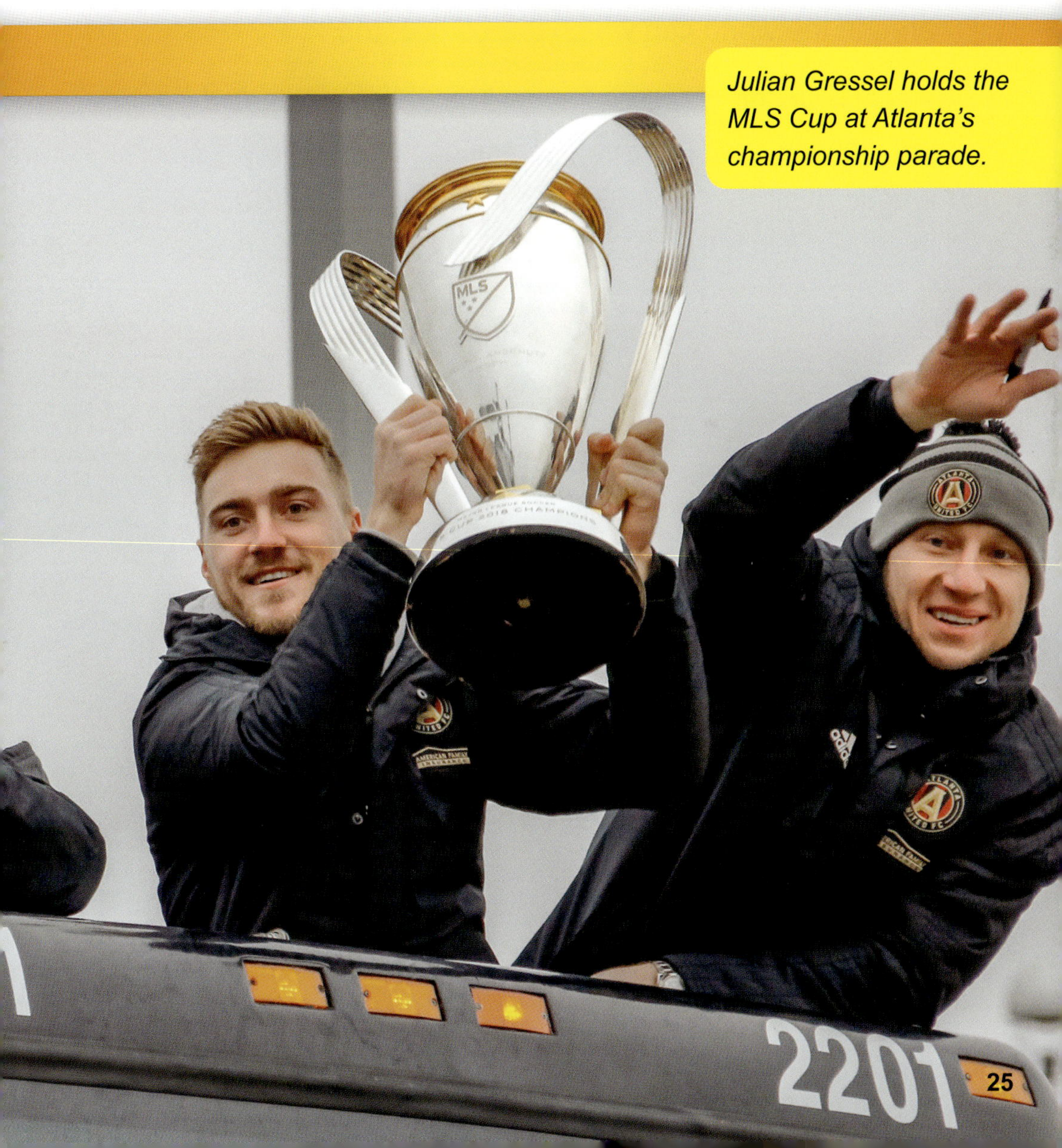

Julian Gressel holds the MLS Cup at Atlanta's championship parade.

Soccer is an old sport. MLS had to catch up with the rest of the world. The league has grown quickly, though. Today it is as popular as ever. In 2005, MLS had twelve teams. By 2019 that number had doubled. More were planned. Average attendance continued to rise. In 2019, Minnesota United opened a new stadium. That made seventeen **soccer-specific stadiums** in MLS. Fans around the world can watch the games, too.

D.C. United was great early. The Los Angeles Galaxy led the way later. Now new teams continue to grow the league. It started slow. But the league has now lived up to its name. It is a truly major league.

Leonardo Bertone, center, celebrates scoring the first goal in FC Cincinnati history on March 2, 2019.

MAPFRE STADIUM

HOME OF THE COLUMBUS CREW

Built: 1999

MAPFRE Stadium hosted its first match on May 15, 1999. It was the first stadium built specifically to host Major League Soccer.

Cost: $28.5 million

The stadium took less than a year to build. Minor improvements have been made over the years.

Capacity: 19,968

The stadium added a concert stage in 2008 that reduced the seating for soccer. It can seat 25,000–30,000 for concerts.

Playing surface: Grass

Most MLS teams play on grass. The few that play on artificial turf usually do so because they share the field with a pro football team.

BEYOND THE BOOK

After reading the book, it's time to think about what you learned. Try the following exercises to jumpstart your ideas.

THINK

THAT'S NEWS TO ME. David Beckham's arrival to MLS was a major story around the world. How might news sources be able to fill in more detail about this? What new information could you find in news articles? Where could you go to find those sources?

CREATE

PRIMARY SOURCES. A primary source is an original document, photograph, or interview. Make a list of different primary sources you might be able to find about MLS. What new information might you learn from these sources?

SHARE

SUM IT UP. Write one paragraph summarizing the important points from this book. Make sure it's in your own words. Don't just copy what is in the text. Share the paragraph with a classmate. Does your classmate have any comments about the summary? Do they have additional questions about MLS?

GROW

REAL-LIFE RESEARCH. What places could you visit to learn more about MLS? What other things could you learn while you were there?

Visit www.ninjaresearcher.com/0707 to learn how to take your research skills and book report writing to the next level!

RESEARCH

SEARCH LIKE A PRO
Learn about how to use search engines to find useful websites.

FACT OR FAKE?
Discover how you can tell a trusted website from an untrustworthy resource.

TEXT DETECTIVE
Explore how to zero in on the information you need most.

SHOW YOUR WORK
Research responsibly—learn how to cite sources.

WRITE

GET TO THE POINT
Learn how to express your main ideas.

PLAN OF ATTACK
Learn prewriting exercises and create an outline.

DOWNLOADABLE REPORT FORMS

Further Resources

BOOKS

Gagne, Tammy. *LA Galaxy*. Mitchell Lane Publishers, 2018.

Kortemeier, Todd. *Superstars of World Soccer*. Amicus High Interest, 2017.

Rausch, David. *Major League Soccer*. Bellwether Media, 2015.

WEBSITES

Factsurfer.com gives you a safe, fun way to find more information.

1. Go to www.factsurfer.com.
2. Enter "Major League Soccer" into the search box and click 🔍.
3. Select your book cover to see a list of related websites.

Glossary

mascot: A mascot is a character who represents a sports team. Timber Joey is one of MLS's most popular mascots.

nutmegged: A defender gets nutmegged when a player passes the ball between his or her legs. Eric Wynalda nutmegged the defender before scoring.

playoffs: The playoffs, in which teams compete for the championship, take place after the regular season. Portland beat Seattle in the playoffs and moved on to the MLS Cup.

rival: A rival is an opponent with which a team has a fierce history. Portland and Seattle are two of MLS's fiercest rivals.

salary cap: A salary cap is a limit on how much teams can pay players. A tight salary cap prevented teams from signing expensive players.

soccer-specific stadiums: In the United States, a stadium designed to primarily host soccer games is called a soccer-specific stadium. Columbus opened the league's first soccer-specific stadium.

traditions: Traditions are customs that people follow. Sawing the "victory log" after a goal is one of Portland's traditions.

Index

PHOTO CREDITS

The images in this book are reproduced through the courtesy of: Jacob Kupferman/Cal Sport Media/AP Images, front cover (center); EFKS/Shuttertstock Images, front cover (background); Marcio Jose Sanchez/AP Images, p. 3; Brett Davis/AP Images, pp. 4–5; TFoxFoto/Shutterstock Images, p. 5; Anatoliy Lukich/Shutterstock Images, p. 7; Red Line Editorial, pp. 8, 27 (chart); Keeton Gale/Shutterstock Images, p. 9 (top); Artyooran/Shutterstock Images, p. 9 (bottom); Michael Caulfield/AP Images, pp. 10–11; Lenny Ignelzi/AP Images, p. 12; Lifestyle Graphic/Shutterstock Images, p. 13; Chris Young/The Canadian Press/AP Images, pp. 14–15; ACHPF/Shutterstock Images, p. 15; Photo Works/Shutterstock Images, p. 16; Steven Senne/AP Images, p. 17; Mark Avery/AP Images, p. 18; Ringo H.W. Chiu/AP Images, p. 20; lev radin/Shutterstock Images, p. 21; Rich von Biberstein/Icon Sportswire/AP Images, pp. 22–23; Todd Kirkland/AP Images, p. 24; Lee Reese/Shutterstock Images, p. 25; Ted S. Warren/AP Images, p. 26; Adam Lacy/Icon Sportswire/AP Images, p. 27 (stadium); Alexander Mak/Shutterstock Images, p. 30.

ABOUT THE AUTHOR

Derek Moon is a writer and an avid Stratego player. He lives in Watertown, Massachusetts, with his wife, daughter, and Boston terrier, Rockafowla.